AFROS, BRAIDS, & CURLS

ABCs FOR *Curly* GIRLS

Daniela J. Lopez: tallgirldani@gmail.com
 @tallgirldani

Christen A. Whyte: chriswhyte4326@yahoo.com
 @darkwhyte

For every girl
that has ever needed a reminder
to love the skin she's in…
myself included

A IS FOR THE AFRO THAT I WEAR LIKE A CROWN.

A

B

B IS FOR THE
BRAIDS
I WEAR THAT NEVER
MAKE ME FROWN.

C

C IS FOR THE
CURLS
AND COILS THAT
SPRING BACK
INTO SHAPE.

D

D IS FOR
DETANGLING
THE KNOTS MY CURLS
CAN MAKE.

E IS FOR THE **ENDS** I GET TRIMMED
EVERY ONCE IN A WHILE.

F IS FOR **FLUFFY**
HAIR SO SOFT IT MAKES ME SMILE.

F

G

G IS FOR THE
GRAVITY
MY HAIR SOMETIMES DEFIES.

H IS FOR THE
HEADSCARF
I PUT ON WHEN NIGHT
REACHES THE SKIES.

I IS FOR
IMAGINING
DIFFERENT STYLES
THAT I CAN WEAR.

J IS FOR THE
JOY
I FEEL BECAUSE I
LOVE MY HAIR!

K

K IS FOR THE
KINKS
MY HAIR HAS,
THEY'RE SIMPLY
TWISTS AND TURNS.

L IS FOR THE
LOCS
I WEAR UP, DOWN,
OR IN BEAUTIFUL
PATTERNS.

M IS FOR
MASSAGING
MY SCALP WITH
CONDITIONER
OR SHAMPOO.

M

N IS FOR
NATURAL HAIR.
I LOVE MINE;
I LOVE YOURS TOO!

O IS FOR THE **OILS** I USE TO KEEP MY HAIR SHINY.

P IS FOR
PUFFS
PONYTAILS THAT ARE CURLY,
COILY, AND FLUFFY.

P

Q

Q IS FOR
QUEEN;

I AM LIGHT,
I AM A STAR.

R IS FOR
RADIANCE.
SHINE BRIGHT
BE PROUD OF WHO
YOU ARE!

S IS FOR

SALON

SOMETIMES I GET MY HAIR DONE THERE.

S

T

T IS FOR THE
TWISTS
**I WEAR TO STYLE OR
LOC MY HAIR.**

U IS FOR

UNIQUE

FOR NO TWO HEADS
ARE QUITE THE SAME.

V IS FOR
VARIETY
SOMETIMES IT'S WILD
SOMETIMES IT'S TAME.

W IS FOR
WATER,
MY NATURAL HAIR'S
BEST FRIEND.

W

X MARKS THE SPECIAL SPOT ON MY HEART THAT NATURAL HAIR HAS PENNED.

Y IS FOR **YOU,**
THE ONLY PERSON YOU CAN BE.

Y

Z IS FOR THE
ZEAL
I HAVE FOR MY HAIR,
IT MAKES ME HAPPY
TO BE ME!

Z

About Author/Illustrator Daniela J. Lopez

Daniela J. Lopez is an art educator, content creator, and hair model. Born and raised in New York City, she has taught visual art to middle and high school students in NYC public schools for over 7 years. After cutting all of her relaxed hair and returning to her natural roots, she created a YouTube channel to support and inspire others with tight coils during their natural hair journey. In 2017, Daniela was featured as a natural hair model in the Texture on the Runway fashion show during New York Fashion Week. Her debut children's book, Afros, Braids, and Curls: ABCs for Curly Girls, is an alphabet book written and illustrated to promote self-love and pride in girls with naturally curly and textured hair.

About Illustrator Christen A. Whyte

Christen A. Whyte is a freelance illustrator from New Jersey. He is a self-taught artist that has been drawing practically his entire life. While his main focus is on both digital and hand-drawn illustrations, he is looking to expand to other mediums. Examples of his work can be seen on his personal Instagram @darkwhyte. He can also be contacted via email at chriswhyte4326@yahoo.com.